The
THIRD
BUCKET

Living It and Filling It

RICHARD COPE
RANDY BRUNSON

outskirtspress

DENVER, COLORADO

Outskirts Press, Inc.
http://www.outskirtspress.com

ISBN: 978-1-4787-4650-8

Outskirts Press and the "OP" logo are trademarks belonging to Outskirts Press, Inc.

PRINTED IN THE UNITED STATES OF AMERICA

Chapter One

Goods and Services

The cars rushing in and out of Research Park played a happy song in Larry's head. The sound meant commerce and consumers—folks hurrying to make and spend money—and this was a good thing. Larry loved to see people unloading cartons of goods through the back doors of buildings and shopping centers early in the morning, and he relished the idea that those things would end up in the hands of people who handed over their hard-earned dollars to a cashier. It was a simple process, trading money for things, and each time it happened, it had to be counted. And that was what Larry lived for.

Larry was a businessman. He worked his way up to the top of the ladder by watching the math of the buying public. He had built his business by believing wholeheartedly that numbers don't lie, and that was all there was to it. His product was as complex as he was simple: a piece of accounting software called CE1 and it was in just about every store in the Southeast that had a cash register.

Larry didn't fool himself into thinking his good fortune was providential, although he did believe that God had a part in it. He was a Christian man, honest and hardworking and scrupulous. He went to church and gave at collection time and raised his children in the faith. When it came time to give to charity, he did it with the same thought that he gave to everything else: it was the right thing to do. It was the right thing to be frugal at home and in business, and this thought comforted Larry on the coldest of days.

"Don't live beyond your means" was a phrase that would elicit groans from his thirtysomething children because they had heard it all their lives, but it was as true as a prayer for Larry Rose Sr., president of Cash Drawer Technologies. The plaque on Larry's office wall read "I Count Everything." And indeed, he did.

This particular morning was a glorious southern summer day, and the sky was blue and scrubbed clean from an early shower. His walk from the sensible sedan that he paid for in cash was a short one up to the front doors of the modest building in Chapel Hill, one point on a triangle that meant everything "tech." This was the bastion of Cash Drawer Technologies, but it looked like any other large, boxy office enclave: windows and stone, not new and not old, with little to let the layperson know it was the headquarters of half the "point-of-sale systems" across the South.

Larry was early for a morning meeting that started prompt-ly at eight o'clock. Another one of his adages (and his were legion) was "If you're not ten minutes early, you're late." Today he walked in the door at seven fifty. And at eight o'clock he was going to meet someone who was about to change his life.

Chapter 2

Policies and Procedures

At the end of a side road, a very still man sat on a rock regarding the sky. The magnolias were heavy with tray-sized blooms, and the scent of one of them made the man smile, pulling him out of his trance. He breathed deeply, stretched his arms above his head, and got off the rock with purpose, looking at his watch: 7:45. It was time. He strode up to the glass doors of Cash Drawer Technologies and pulled them open, meeting the receptionist with a benevolent smile.

"I'm here to see Mr. Rose," he said.

The receptionist performed a rehearsed but not inauthentic response: "Do you have an appointment?"

It wasn't her fault—this man looked more like a summer intern than the reason for what Mr. Rose's assistant called a "very private meeting".

"Yes, I'm Jack Stock. He's expecting me."

"Of course, Mr. Stock." Although this kind of mistake usually ruffled the girl, the man's warm tone allowed her to recover gracefully. "I'll let him know you are here." She walked down the hall and swung open a huge oak door, asking Jack to follow her.

"You are welcome to sit here while I go get him. Would you like something to drink?" she asked, although it came out sounding like "drank," due to her Carolina accent. He said water would be just fine. He sat on a yellow and white striped chair while he watched the mourning doves on the wires across the street. They jockeyed awkwardly, bobbing and flapping, until some invisible force drove them to burst into flight, their wings singing.

The sound of sure footsteps on the polished floors announced the arrival of Mr. Rose, who strode into the room beaming. His smile creased his cheeks as he jutted out one arm for a handshake and another for a pat on Jack's back. "Pleased to meet you, Jack!" he said in his elegant drawl. "So glad you were able to make your way over here this morning. Please have a seat."

"Oh, it's my pleasure, Mr. Rose. I've heard great things about you," Jack offered warmly as he sat back down.

Larry launched right into the reason for the meeting. "Well, Jack, you know I have built this business from the ground up, from scratch, and I'm sure you can understand how much that means to me." He didn't wait for a reply. "Naturally, I have always thought I would sell it when it was time to retire. But the thought of handing Cash Drawer off to some other company makes me queasy. And I want to do something special with it, something meaningful. So I started thinking about a succession plan, handing it off to the kids when the time is right. On the other hand, selling it would give me a chance to make a difference in the world, maybe give some of the proceeds to charity of some sort."

"I'm in a quandary, Jack. I can't do both. So when I told Bud what I was thinking, he told me to get in touch with you, said you had all kinds of ideas. Bud's my best friend so I couldn't say no, right?"

"That's what best friends are for," Jack suggested.

"I guess so," Larry said with a shake of his silver hair. "I have been in this industry a long time. Before I was even born, my father and his business partner started US Cash Machines, and they literally wrote the book on sales strategies." His eyes got wide. "They built the best sales force in history. It was like boot camp for sales execs, and everybody who came out of that training program was a wiz at converting sales. Those same ideas have been copied by every major company in the world! Did you know that?"

"No, I sure didn't, Mr. Rose."

Jack's measured answer brought Larry back to earth. "Well, it's important because I built Cash Drawer on the same principles," he explained.

"Yes, it's good to know the history, and you do seem quite proud of it, Mr. Rose. Please continue. The more I know, the more I can help you make the right decisions."

"Please call me Larry. How much time do these transactions usually take?"

"As much time as you want, Larry. These things are not measured in minutes but in moments, which are very different, you see." Jack looked expectantly at his new friend.

"I don't see, but you've definitely got my attention," Larry said, more serious now. "Where do we start?"

The rest of the morning was spent in comfortable conversation, with Larry getting a chance to talk about the history of the company, all the way from adding machines and cash registers to how his engineers invented handheld devices the size of a stick of chewing gum that can handle bundles of data in mind-blowing dimensions. Jack listened with the innocent attention of a child but asked questions that showed he was piecing together more than just information. At some point, Grace, Larry's assistant, asked them if they were hungry and came back with pimento cheese sandwiches from the shop down the street. They washed them down with sweet tea, which Jack said was delicious.

"You haven't had my wife's sweet tea," Larry countered. "It's the best in the Carolinas, maybe the world. Why don't you come over for dinner this week and you can meet her?"

"You're very gracious, Larry. I would like to meet your wife. What's her name?"

"Eloise since the day she was born, but I just call her Ellie. I will let her know we are having a guest at the house, and we can nail down the date later. It will be good for you two to meet since she's got an interest in the business as well. Like I always say, half of mine is hers, and the other half is hers, too!"

Larry stood up to his full six feet and wrapped his arm around Jack, who said with genuine fondness, "Thank you for the sandwiches and the tea. I look forward to coming to your house for dinner."

"I'll have my assistant give you a call on Monday. Is there a certain number she should call?"

Jack gave Larry his business card. "All my information is on there," he said, as he waved good-bye over his shoulder.

"Hmm," Larry said a minute later, turning the card over in his hand. All it said was JACK STOCK.

"Pretty simple guy," he muttered to himself. He put the

card in his wallet and promptly forgot about Jack. Lawrence T. Rose Sr. was heading home for the weekend. He walked with a spring in his step to the car and pointed it north toward home. He was suddenly thirsty for a glass of Ellie's sweet tea.

Chapter 3

Dogs and Tomatoes

On Monday morning Grace did indeed set up dinner arrangements for Tuesday evening at six o'clock. She gave Jack the address and directions to the Roses' house on Sycamore Street and told him to dress casual. On Tuesday afternoon, Jack put his hand through his sandy hair, looked down at his white shirt and khakis, and nodded to himself.

His walk afforded him the pleasure of marveling at the crape myrtles lined up along the private drive, the end of which sported an intricate wrought iron gate. The center of the gate held a carving of a rose in dark wood, and inside blinked a barely detectable camera lens. As Jack took his next step, the gate glided open with a whisper.

The estate was laid out like a horseshoe, with the driveway cutting a swath in front of the brick home. Pale yellow irises, the exact shade of the paint on the house's tasteful columns and trim, waved in the breeze. On one whole side of the horseshoe was a bank of windows, and it was through a black lacquered door beside them that a woman emerged, a dish towel in her hand.

"You must be Jack!" she said as she held out her arms. "I'm so glad you could make it. Come on in out of the heat for heaven's sake; I've got some ice-cold tea for you."

Two golden labs met him inside the door and wagged their tails furiously as they licked his ankles.

"Petunia! Azalea! Let the man be!" Ellie called without a bit of authority. "They smile with their tails," she said, "so they must be smiling like mad at you!" They followed Jack, trotting behind him.

All four of them walked down the hall of windows along a shining black-and-white tiled floor. Every other window was punctuated by huge potted palms that spread their fronds as though inviting them into the next room. Ellie sat him down in the parlor on a tufted yellow sofa and handed him a glass from a tray on the coffee table. The dogs put a chin on each of his knees.

"That there is the most refreshing drink in the world! I should have bottled it!" boomed Larry as he entered the room. "How are you, Jack?"

"Thank you both very much for inviting me. The tea is great," he said.

"It's a secret family recipe." Ellie smiled slyly as she slipped into the kitchen.

"Yeah, there's more security on that than on my software," joked Larry.

"Dinner's in five minutes!" they heard from the kitchen a second later.

They sat down in the dining room to a meal of pork chops and corn pudding with a fresh tomato salad. It all looked mouthwatering. But as soon as Jack had his napkin folded on his lap, his host got down to business. Larry talked about how he prided himself on making decisions based on facts and figures. He had to have hard data on everything before he "put the hammer down," as he said.

"So when I asked Bud if I should sell the business or hand it down to the kids, Bud said one thing: 'Jack Stock. He may not look like much, but he will change your life.'"

"So, Jack," said Larry, layering a piece of pork tenderly on top of a forkful of corn pudding, "how are you going to change my life?"

"I'm not," said Jack. "You are."

Jack continued, contemplating a slice of tomato. "Mrs. Rose, these are very good."

"Oh, aren't you sweet," she said as a statement of fact. "I grew them myself right out back!"

"Yes, my Ellie is very self-sufficient. We may have been blessed with wealth, but she doesn't believe in people doing for her." He said this with true fondness but was beginning to feel he was losing control of the conversation. Shaking his silver head to get back on track, he plunged ahead.

"Okay. So how am I going to change my life then?"

Chapter 4

Tithes and Offerings

"Do you think it needs changing?" Jack asked.

"Well, I don't know. I never really thought about it before." He rolled the question over in his mind. "I guess change is good if it comes for the right reasons."

"And what would those reasons be?"

"Well, I don't like change just for change's sake. Some things are better left the way they are—the Bible—for instance. I'd say that's a pretty good example of something that doesn't need any changing, at least not in my mind," he said.

"Oh yes," Ellie interjected. "We both do. I teach Bible study to the youngsters in the congregation, and Larry teaches it to the older ones. We have spent many hours discussing our lessons on the scriptures. He is quite a scholar in his own right," she beamed.

"Yes," Larry said, "you'd be surprised how many youngsters don't know the first thing about tithing, for instance. Did you know that Hebrew scholars say that tithing in the Jewish tradition shows up some five centuries before Moses? Of course you know the word tithe comes from a derivative of the number 'ten,' and it means that we Christians should be giving a tenth of all we have to the Lord."

Ellie rose to the occasion as if she was teaching Bible class. "I teach my little ones that tithes and offerings support the church and help the poor."

"Why do you think they pass around a plate during the church service?" Jack asked.

"Well," Larry reflected, "you can give anytime. It's part of the church service because it is considered an act of worship. When Christians put money in the plate, they are worshipping God according to his word in the Bible."

"So Christians give to the poor and needy because they are following God's law?" Jack asked.

"Yep, and we give proudly, don't we, Ellie?" Larry reached over and squeezed her hand.

"And that's because it is expected of you?" Jack continued.

Larry said, "Well we want to give. We are happy to give. We don't just do it because we are told to. We are blessed to know that our money goes to the kingdom and to charities and helps hundreds of people."

"The Bible says 'The Lord loves a cheerful giver'!" Ellie sang.

"Ellie and Larry," Jack began, the echo of Ellie's voice in his head, "it sounds like being generous fills you both with joy." They nodded. "What would happen if you gave more than ten percent —would you have even more joy?"

Chapter 5

Cake and Buckets

"**O**h, I know what you're getting at, Jack, but from someone like me, ten percent is still a heck of a lot! And remember, people like us—successful business owners—end up giving a big chunk to Uncle Sam." Larry jabbed his thumb in the air as if to indicate that Uncle Sam was just in the next room.

When he saw Jack's confused look, he settled himself in his chair and began to explain.

"See, Jack, I look at my money like this: You have two buckets. One is the lifestyle bucket. You put money in there for the way you want to live your life—your home, your possessions, food on the table, those kinds of things. If you work hard, you get to send your kids to college, shop for nice things, and go on a vacation now and then with your lovely bride." He winked at Mrs. Rose, who was clearing the dishes, and she flashed him a sweet smile.

"Then," he continued, "you have the second bucket. That's the tax bucket."

Jack leaned in, very interested, and told Larry to continue.

"That bucket," Larry said with a resigned grimace, "is for our good friends in the government. As much as I don't like it, it's a fact of life—and the only thing besides death you can be sure of in this world. Right, Jack?"

Jack nodded slowly and said, "So you don't feel the same way about this bucket as you feel about the other bucket?"

"Did you get heat stroke out there, Jack? We want to keep that bucket as low as possible!"

Ellie was cutting into a coconut cake. As she placed a slice on a plate and handed it to Jack, she said, "Of course we are grateful for what we have already."

"What would you do if you could put less in the tax bucket?" Jack asked innocently.

Larry regarded Jack with a wary frown. He was beginning to wonder what Jack knew about business finances. "Legally, there are only so many ways to skin a cat, you know."

"Okay, but let's say it's legal and ethical. Then would you?"

"Well, yeah, but that would be quite a trick, Jack. I can't imagine how it would work."

Jack brushed some coconut crumbs from his whiskerless

chin and looked fondly at Larry and Ellie. "Imagination is what I do best. If you leave that part up to me, I think I can help you."

This wasn't the first time that Larry thought there was something odd—but undeniably riveting—about their guest. Jack didn't seem to be a financial expert, and Larry was beginning to wonder how he was going to help with the very serious matter of what to do with Cash Drawer Technologies. But on the other hand, Jack seemed to have answers to questions Larry hadn't even thought of yet.

"I'm no stranger to imagination, Jack," he said. "Cash Drawer has some of the best working practices in the country: flex time, award-winning day care centers, free snacks to all our workers. We imagined what would build loyalty and productivity, and it worked!"

"It also sounds like you care about your employees," said Jack. "I'm happy to hear that."

Long after the last bite of cake was eaten, Larry and Jack stayed at the table talking. When they moved to the parlor for one more glass of sweet tea, Ellie asked Jack if he had far to go that night to get home.

"No, Mrs. Rose, it will only take me a few minutes, but I should be getting back soon." He looked at his watch.

"Well, I expect to see you at my office bright and early tomorrow morning," Larry said as he walked Jack to the front door. "Is nine o'clock okay?"

"I will be there, Larry. And thank you both for a wonderful dinner."

"Oh, it was our pleasure!" Ellie said. "I hope you come again soon."

"Now that you have had some of Ellie's cooking, you know why I married her," Larry joked.

"One of many very good reasons," Jack said.

"What a fascinating and sweet man!" Ellie remarked as she brought in the dogs.

"Ellie," Larry said, "I can't figure him out. I'm not exactly sure he knows what he's doing."

Chapter 6

Caesar and Larry

The day would be full of meetings and appointments for Larry, who drove from his handsome Chapel Hill home to the office park deep in thought. He would be meeting with his accountant to discuss financials, and something in the accountant's memo suggested that there might be some unpleasant news. Larry had spent thirty years raising the business "from a pup," as he liked to say, and certainly sweat equity was part of the package. Retiring was not going to be easy. He wondered if anyone really understood that.

Jack saw his reflection in the glass doors of Cash Drawer Technologies and ran his fingers through his hair before entering the lobby. The receptionist remembered him and walked him down to the lounge to wait.

Larry's face seemed to have a few more creases in it than it did last night.

"Well, Jack," he said as a hello, "I just got some sobering news." He poured a cup of coffee from a silver carafe on his desk and handed it to Jack. "I have spent thirty years building this company, and my CPA just let me know that if I retire and sell it now, I'll have to pay twenty-five percent of that in capital gains taxes. That's like seven years of growth right down the drain!"

"Into the tax bucket?" Jack asked over his coffee cup.

"Yep. 'Render under Caesar what is Caesar's...' There's no way around it. If I sell the company, the lovely folks over at the IRS see that as income—a lot of income. But you know that; you are the financial advisor here."

"Did Bud tell you that?"

Larry frowned. "Well, no, but I figured. Granted, you do not fit the profile, and you haven't given me any advice yet, but you are an advisor, right?"

"Yes, I am an advisor." Jack smiled.

"Well, good then." Larry applied himself to the file folder in front of him. "Let me show you something." He pulled out sheets of paper with pie charts and columns and slid them across the table. "Right now our revenue is about ten million. And many folks value a company like ours around the same as the revenue, so our valuation is around ten million dollars also. In addition to my salary, I get about one million dollars in K-1 income," Larry said.

"Larry, you mentioned that you write checks for charity, right?"

"Right, from our lifestyle bucket, if you want to think of it that way. Every year we decide who we want to give to— the Humane Society, United Way, organizations like that. That's what most people do."

"How much of your net worth is in cash assets?"

Larry thought for a minute. "I would say about ten percent," he mused.

"But doesn't that seem strange? I mean your business and everything else has the other ninety percent."

"What are you getting at?" Larry said.

"The money you are giving to charity is coming out of the lifestyle bucket. What if it came out of the tax bucket?"

"Jack, I have lived my whole life counting everything. And I can't see any way to give to charity with noncash assets!"

"Larry," Jack said, "are you a business owner?"

"Of course I am," Larry said with conviction.

"Then you can."

Chapter 7

Simple Syrup and Fancy Cars

Ellie took a large glass measuring bowl out of the cupboard and placed six tea bags in it. She poured boiling water over them and let them steep while she made the simple syrup. Then she poured it through a sieve into the tea, and set the whole thing on the counter to cool.

The phone rang.

It was Bill Stanton, one of the volunteers at the church. He wanted to confirm her Sunday school teaching schedule. Ellie wasn't a judgmental person—and hoped she wasn't being one now—but she did notice that Bill was one of those people who arrived at church in a fancy car. He parked next to other fancy cars. She honestly appreciated his gift of time volunteering for the church, and it was for this reason that she was able to be kind and polite, but in the back of her mind she thought that money he spent on other things could go back into the ministry and help others. Having served on the board at the church, she happened to know that he was among the few who weren't very generous at the end of the year. It was like pulling teeth to get him to give anything, according to the stories she heard from the fund-raising committee. He was definitely not a "cheerful giver," she surprised herself by thinking.

When Larry got home that evening, Ellie mentioned Bill's call but didn't confide her musings on how he spent his money. She took the pitcher of completely cooled sweet tea out of the refrigerator and poured Larry a glass. He drank it with gusto, which made Ellie smile, despite her recent irritation with Bob.

"Larry," Ellie began, "do you think it's possible to give more than ten percent of our earnings each year?"

Larry all but rounded on Ellie. "Did Jack talk to you today?"

"No, but I just can't get our talk out of my mind," she said.

"Yeah, he seems to have that effect on people."

Ellie looked at her husband. He was rarely sullen. He looked back at Ellie with affection, but she could tell he was bothered by something important. He looked awfully worn out for a Monday, and his whole face seemed to knot up right between his brows.

"What's the matter?" she asked.

"I don't know, Ellie. I'm all mixed up."

Ellie had known Larry a long time, and he rarely got "mixed up." When he did, he certainly didn't like to admit it. "That's not like you," she offered.

"Well, usually I know what's going on! I think everybody is out to get me today. First, Hank Rogers told me I might as well throw seven years of my business right in the city dump, and then I met with Jack, and he tried to convince me to give it away…"

"What?"

"I don't know exactly what he was getting at, but he told me that most people only give to charities and things from about ten percent of their worth because the other ninety percent is tied up in assets. But here's the kicker: he told me a story about some pharmaceutical company that was about to go public…but instead they gave half their business to charity! I thought that was very nice of them, but I'll be darned if I'm going to do any such thing—"

"I thought you were going to retire and either sell it or hand if off to the kids," Ellie interrupted. "What did you tell him?"

"I wanted to tell him he was off his rocker," Larry said sheepishly. "But just at that moment, my next appointment arrived and we had to put off our talk. All he said after that was to think about the story and, if I was so inclined, to take a look at Philippians chapter four, verses six and seven."

"I know that one." Ellie smiled. "I taught it to my Sunday school students. 'Do not be anxious about anything.'"

Chapter 8

Assets and Trout

At their nine o'clock meeting the following day, Larry was significantly less creased in the eyebrows. They were talking about appreciated assets, a favorite subject of Larry's.

"Anyone," Jack was saying, "who is planning to sell an appreciated asset — securities, real estate, interest in a privately owned business like yours — can avoid capital gains taxes with careful planning and foresight."

"Okay," Larry said, "but what if I don't want to sell the business?"

"That's where the magic comes in," said Jack. "What if you could keep control of it and generate income at significantly lower tax rates that you could then give away?"

"Not possible."

"A lot of people don't know that this is possible. But it is. Let me show you."

Jack took a large marker from the white board on the paneled walls of the boardroom and drew a rough picture of a bucket. He looked back at Larry and smiled. "I really like your idea of the two buckets, so let's use them here." Jack wrote "Taxes" on the bucket.

"You'd like to pay less in taxes. Right, Larry?"

Larry's eyebrows suggested this was a silly question.

"And," he said, "you are a generous man. Right?"

Larry made an audible harrumph and said, "Yes."

"You like to give to the causes you believe in?"

"Of course."

"Well then, you are going to love this."

Jack drew another bucket and labeled it "Lifestyle." Above the buckets he drew a large rectangle and wrote "Cash Drawer" on it. "Here's your business. Okay, Larry?"

Clearly this guy did not go to art school, Larry found himself thinking. But he smiled and said, "Okay. And it's worth about ten million dollars, remember."

"So," Jack continued, "out of that ten-million-dollar business you receive a salary and one million dollars in K-1 income."

Jack wrote the amounts in the buckets, turned to Larry, and said, "Okay. This is one scenario."

He ran his hand through his sandy hair before picking up the eraser from the tray on the white board. And then he said, grinning, "Here's a different scenario, Larry. This is going to blow your mind."

Jack picked up his marker and drew a third bucket. He labeled it "Giving." In that bucket he wrote "$300,000 a year."

"Wait a minute, how are you managing that?" Larry barked.

Jack's eyes were sparkling. "You give something away to get it."

"What are you talking about? And what does all this have to do with Cash Drawer?"

Jack was practically jumping up and down. "Remember when we talked about cash and noncash assets yesterday, Larry?"

"I sure do. But I still don't understand what you are driving at there."

"Let's assume that your ten-million-dollar business was represented by ten shares of stock and you now own them all. If you gave three shares of stock or thirty percent of your company to a donor-advised fund, you'd get a three-million-dollar write-off against your income, correct?"

"Hold on, Speedy. Did I hear you say thirty percent of my company?" Larry looked thoroughly confused. "You want me to give away part of my business?"

"That's why I'm here, Larry."

"What do you mean?"

Jack put the markers down, walked over to where Larry was sitting, and looked at him. "There is a reason Bud told you to meet with me. I am here to tell you my story. And, if you let me, I can help you give more than you and Ellie ever dreamed possible." He put a hand on Larry's shoulder. "But you have to have courage. And you have to have faith."

Larry stood up. Once again, time had flown by in the presence of Jack Stock. His next appointment was ready. He still had a whole day of work left, but he was reluctant to have to wait until the next morning to hear Jack's story.

"Jack, Ellie and I are going out to dinner tonight. Would you like to join us? I can call the restaurant and change the reservation to three, and then you can tell us both."

"I am grateful for the invitation, but I think you and Ellie need this time alone. I want to make sure you understand what I am saying before we go any further. I am asking you to give away part of your business."

At Larry's slow inhale, Jack gave him a warm smile and continued. "I can tell that you and your wife talk about things together—that you value her opinions and she respects yours. You can't have a real heart-to-heart with me there. You two talk it over tonight and see how you feel, and we'll see each other in the morning."

Of course Larry knew he was right; he was just being impatient, and Jack had certainly picked up on the fact that he never made a big decision without being in sync with Ellie about it first. A good-natured laugh bubbled up when he realized how transparent that was.

"Okay, Jack, you win! But sometime you have to come out to the Carolina Inn with us. I don't like to spend money on restaurants when I have a wife who cooks like Ellie, but one can only go so long without their Carolina trout. Best in the state."

He clapped Jack on the back and walked him down the hall. The doors were gleaming in the morning light and made him squint, wrinkling the corners of his eyes. But the frown seemed to have smoothed between his brows. He opened the door for Jack, who thanked him for his time and walked out into the clear blue day.

Chapter 9

Talks and Walks

On the way home, after a very busy day, Larry realized that he was looking forward to talking to Ellie. Part of his reason for taking her out to their favorite restaurant was due to the fact that he knew he had been a bit preoccupied lately. And he never wanted her to think that she didn't come first.

He pulled into the driveway of their home, just off Rosemary Street, and put the car in the garage. "I'm home!" he announced. Ellie had already guessed this by the way Azalea and Petunia bounded to the door. "I'm ready!" she answered. "I was thinking we could walk there; it's such a beautiful night!"

"You read my mind," he said, chuckling. "I already put the car in the garage."

Their neighborhood, with its stately oaks, green glades,

and deer padding through the lawns, was only a few blocks from the bustling college town of Chapel Hill, but it felt like a different world, and they loved it—once Ellie figured out how to keep the deer from making a buffet out of her garden, that is. It was indeed a beautiful evening, still early, and Ellie practically swooned at the flowers blooming along Franklin Street. Larry was tickled pink at the thought of not having to pay for valet parking.

The Crossroads Restaurant, in the historic Carolina Inn, was literally at the crossroads of two streets: Columbia and Cameron. They had been coming here for years and celebrated many an accomplishment with their children, Molly and Mitch, who had been students at the University of North Carolina. The restaurant had experienced many transformations, but they thought this was by far the best. The chef offered up succulent southern fare, for which their stroll had made them especially hungry.

The dining room was decorated in Carolina blue, and ficus trees in huge ceramic pots lined the halls outside. It was no accident that Ellie felt right at home here. "I'm so glad we came out to dinner tonight, Larry." Her cheeks were rosy with a healthy glow. "I feel like it's a special occasion!"

Larry looked at his pretty bride and grinned like a schoolboy. "I feel that way, too, Ellie."

After ordering, he launched into an account of his morning meeting with Jack and found himself talking about the anxious feelings he had been experiencing. "Ellie, I think I'm at a crossroads. I feel as if there is something important I am supposed to be doing…and I think it may have something to do with giving more. Does that sound crazy to you?"

"I have been thinking about the same thing." Ellie talked about her feelings regarding the folks at church, the ones who had fancy things but didn't contribute much. "I think those people are controlled by their money when it should be the other way around", added Larry.

Ellie and the kids had heard this speech before. Larry made sure that the family had adhered to the idea that financial freedom comes from not being ruled by money. "That's why I want to give more," she said, "but I am not sure how we can go about it. I was thinking that the sale of the business could help us with that."

"Me, too, but Jack is talking about not selling. You and I always dreamed of handing down the business to Mitch and Molly, and I don't want anything to jeopardize that. Jack asked me to have faith, Ellie."

"Do you?"

He lifted his fork to his lips and chewed on a mustard seed. "Well, part of me is scared. Heck, I don't even know what Jack is talking about!"

"Well, tell me again what he wants you to do."

"He wants us to give part of our interests in the business to some kind of fund. He says this is the whole reason Bud told me to meet him, and you know Bud would never steer me wrong."

Ellie nodded.

Larry went on. "He said he could help us give more than we ever dreamed possible. He told me to talk it over with you and that he had a story to tell me tomorrow...oh, and to have courage."

They had finished their Carolina trout. The waiter, while gathering their cleaned plates, asked if they cared for dessert, to which they replied yes in unison. Larry ordered the Red Velvet cake; Ellie decided on the ice cream trio.

"That way we can share," she justified. Back to her task, she looked at Larry with a calm face. "Honey, I trust Bud, and, for some reason, I trust Jack. I think you should keep an open mind about all this and see where it leads."

Their desserts came—his was a dome of cake and mousse in a puddle of cream, and hers sported three scoops of ice cream in a cookie basket. Larry held up his spoon and clinked it with Ellie's in a sort of toast.

"Okay then," he said. "I will be seeing Jack again tomorrow. And I will try to keep an open mind."

Chapter 10

Giving and Misgivings

Jack went to the board again. He drew three buckets and labeled them Living, Giving, and Taxes.

"Remember at our last meeting we agreed that your business is worth ten million dollars, represented by ten shares of stock?"

Larry nodded.

"And that if you gave three shares of stock—or thirty percent of your company—to a donor-advised fund, you'd get a three-million-dollar write-off against your income?"

"Of course."

"So your company generates one million dollars of K-1 income to you, and the K-1 income distributed to the shareholders is on a pro rata basis, right?"

"Every quarter," said Larry.

"So then every quarter the thirty percent of your company—or the three shares you gave to the donor-advised fund—would get seventy-five thousand dollars, or three hundred thousand dollars a year, right?"

"I guess so," said Larry hesitantly.

"Then watch this." Jack went to the board and pointed to the lifestyle bucket . "This goes *up* because of the three-million-dollar tax deduction for giving the thirty percent of your company away…and because your K-1 income has been reduced, your tax bucket goes *down*. Thirty percent of the K-1 income can now go to a donor-advised fund"—he pointed to the giving bucket—"and your giving bucket now has three hundred thousand dollars a year, at significantly lower tax rates, for you to give away."

"Okay, hold on. First of all, what's a donor-advised fund?" Larry asked.

"It means you, the donor, can advise where the funds go."

"Well, that sounds good. Is it a foundation of some sort?"

"It can be, or some financial institutions have a DAF arm. Either way, they tailor your donations to go to whatever charities or nonprofits you want to contribute to. Also, they handle all the paperwork and things. Oh, and if you want, you can tell them you want to be an anonymous donor," Jack said.

A cloud seemed to come over Larry's eyes. "Jack, I'm not sure I've been honest with you. I don't know how to say this, but the more I think about retiring— even if I save a ton of money on taxes, hand it off to the kids, or whatever—I'm just not sure I can ever be happy just sitting around the club playing golf. Heck, I don't even like golf..." he trailed off.

"Larry, if you do this, you won't lose your grip on your company. You would still have enough ownership in the business to stay in control and never have to retire if you don't want to."

Larry cocked his head, still skeptical.

Jack sat down next to him and poured them both a cup of steaming hot coffee. "I believe I promised you something. And I should have thought of this before I got so excited. I think it's time I told you my story." He rubbed his head and combed his hair with his fingers.

"Well, about five years ago, I owned a carpentry business. You know, cabinets and things for kitchens—fine wood, painstaking craftsmanship. We were growing and things were good. Then one day, out of the blue, I got a call from Kitchen Storage Solutions. They wanted to buy my company!"

Larry's eyebrows shot up.

"You know how people say their life flashes before their

eyes?" Jack asked. "Well, the life of my business flashed before mine — from building things in my dad's garage to owning stores in four states — and now the biggest kitchen retailer in the country was calling me! That's when I remembered something. My dad told me that if I was ever going to sell my business to talk to his friend Randolph Mays first."

"Randolph Mays? The one with the all those tech companies?"

"The very same, although I didn't know that then."

"Gosh, Jack, he's done more for the kingdom than anybody around here."

"Yes, he has. But at the time, I was not aware of all that. Actually, I wasn't aware of much of anything. I wasn't involved with my fellow man, or my church. I was mostly involved with growing my business. I was at a crossroads, Larry. I didn't know it, but the sale of my business opened a huge door for me. It was time for me to change my ideas about money, to change my whole life…"

"Go on, Jack," Larry urged.

"I had to come to terms with what it meant to have the blessing of a sound business and lots of money to buy things. I had to face the fact that I was giving at church because I thought I was supposed to and tried to give the least that I could because I had my priorities mixed up. I gave to charities at Christmastime when I felt guilty for having all the stuff I had, writing checks and then giving those receipts to my CPA. I put money in the basket at church but didn't even think about it. I wasn't greedy, really, because I had the spirit of giving inside me somewhere. It took someone like Randolph to find it in me, and I am forever grateful to him."

"What happened when you met Randolph Mays?"

"Well, first, I listened to his story. Randolph owned a successful and fast-growing company that he loved. He equally loved his mission trips to Central America, where he helped entrepreneurs and farmers raise their standards of living, put their kids in school, and get access to safe drinking water."

"This mission work required funding. Doing it with after-tax revenue is difficult and expensive. So he did two things. First, he brought on a president to help run the company while he was away—he didn't have any kids to hand it down to. Second, he used the same tenacity that he used to build this company to find a better solution to the funding challenge. People told him that when he sold the company one day, they could help him avoid taxes, but that didn't help because he wanted to keep the company. So after a year or two of research, meetings, and phone calls with countless investment advisors, CPAs, tax attorneys, and anyone else he could find, he finally worked out a solution."

"He gave forty-nine percent of his company to a donor-advised fund that would work with privately held assets.

That meant that every quarter income from this company would flow into the donor-advised fund, and he could then direct this income to fund his mission work in Central America. This gave him the financial strength to be able to transition, as he calls it, 'from success to significance.' He was successful as a CEO, and now he wanted to use that success—all his skill, knowledge, and training, plus the financial resources flowing from his company through the donor-advised fund—to help change the world."

"And the rest is history, as they say," Larry said as he leaned back in his chair. "That's pretty inspiring, Jack. So what did you end up doing with your company?"

"I did something very similar. I had always wanted to do something more than just run the company, and I realized it would require financial resources and my own transformation 'from success to significance'…but I didn't know how to get it set up. After hearing Randolph's story, I came back and sat down with my kids. We gave thirty-five percent of our company to a donor-advised fund and the rest to the kids. They now run the company successfully, generating income that flows into my donor-advised fund at significantly lower tax rates. Those funds now give me the ability to drill wells in South America to provide fresh water to poor people.

"But you know what's just as important to me?"

Larry waited for the answer.

"The opportunity to spend time with folks like you. Having watched what Randolph did in his transformation from success to significance, I knew I wanted to do the same. My heart called me to try to help other business owners do the same."

"Jack, didn't people think you were a bit loony, giving away part of your business?"

"Oh yes; especially my own financial advisor! But I had to remember that this was all new to him. How many of his clients were trying to give away thirty-five percent of their company? He soon learned that the people in the foundation were experts in tax law. They do this kind of thing every day."

"When I realized that I could make more of an impact this way than writing checks to charity whenever the mood hit me, I was unstoppable. That was over five years ago, and since that time, I have been helping others, those who are willing to listen and grow. People like you and Ellie, and Bud, who have the spirit of giving woven into their very character."

"Is Bud selling his business?"

"No, but he wants to stop giving from an emotional standpoint. He, like you and Ellie, already has a feeling that there's something bigger out there than just putting money in the hat on Sunday morning and giving to charities at Christmas."

Larry grinned. "So those questions you were asking at our house about tithes and——"

"I wanted to find out what your feelings were about giving."

"That was sneaky, Jack."

"I know." He laughed. "But I wanted to make sure you had faith, even as much as a seed, before we went on this journey together. I have found that it is the only thing we really need to make a difference in this world."

Larry thought about this for a minute. "I guess I need to find myself a financial advisor," he finally said.

Chapter 11

Stocks and Family Bonds

Hank Rogers's office was down a side road in Chapel Hill, flanked on each side by arching redbuds. Larry and Ellie had looked in earnest for a financial planner and finally decided on Hank—partly because of his "living room approach." At their first appointment, he led them into his office, which didn't look like an office at all. There were no desks, no file cabinets, and no boardroom table; it looked more like a living room than a place to crunch numbers. Cream-colored damask armchairs circled a warm oak coffee table, which held, appropriately enough, a china coffee service and a plate of sweet rolls. Instantly they felt at home, and Ellie said so.

"This is my story room," Hank announced proudly. "I wanted a quiet place without distractions and interruptions. No telephones, no fax machines, and no computers! This is where we talk and listen to each other. I call it the 'living room approach': you come to a financial planner to talk about money, but you end up talking about living. It's not just about your finances, you know; it's about your life story."

"But we do get to the planning, right?" Larry asked. "The money part?" He was happy that Ellie liked the decor, and he trusted Hank, but he wanted solid information.

"Eventually," Hank promised. "All in good time."

On this morning, the light through the pines gave the story room a distinctly cozy tone. Once again, the lack of office supplies was noticeable but for the small notepad Hank rested on his ample lap. After they settled in, and Larry and Ellie had time to sip their coffee, Hank said, "Larry, I want to find out all about you and Cash Drawer Technologies. How did you get started? Give me the whole story, soup to nuts." He sat back, a cup of coffee in one hand and the other reaching out, giving Larry the floor.

Larry held forth like a one-man show. He described his younger years as a salesman at US Cash Machines and then the decision to launch out on his own, employing some of the same sales practices he had learned at US Cash Machines.

Hank gently interrupted the flow of Larry's thoughts by asking how he got the money to build a new business from the ground up.

Larry looked at Hank plainly, "I borrowed it."

"Go on," Hank prodded.

"Well, it was a hard decision," Larry reflected. "Ellie and I were newlyweds, and leaving the company was a huge risk, but I saw the writing on the wall. When bar code scanners came out in the seventies, I knew the next wave was computers— and there was some serious money to be made! I was a young buck just at the start of my life. So I jumped right in!"

"And your not-so-young grandfather jumped right in with you," Ellie said and laughed.

"That's right," Larry continued. "He did. My dad's dad was a self-made man and proud of it. He used to tell us stories of his trip to America from Germany on a ship called the *Childe Harold*. With a few coins in his pocket and a lot of determination, he opened up a grocery store on the Lower East Side and for twenty-seven years made an honest living, raised a family, and saved for the future. He managed his life and his accounts scrupulously. So when it came time to take out a loan to start my business, he was the one I went to."

"He knew he could trust you," Ellie beamed.

"Yes, and I knew that I could trust him, too. I was pretty sure he could afford the investment and would treat it like the business transaction that it was—no baggage. And," he explained to Hank, who was perched in his armchair enjoying the tale, "he had the kind of entrepreneurial business sense that I respected. So I asked him for the seed money, and we worked out a contract for me to pay him back. Best decision I ever made."

"So that's how Cash Drawer got started. Did you pay him back?" Hank asked.

"Yes, and then some. He had equity in the company and voting rights. I am thankful—not just for the leg up but for his good advice. His money got things going, but his wisdom served me for well over thirty-five years."

"So it sounds like these things are important to you, Larry: the entrepreneurial spirit, impeccable accounting, and generosity—both financial and," he searched for the right word, "inspirational. Do I have that about right?"

"Yes, yes, that's exactly right. I do value those things. But," Larry said, suddenly looking like he'd landed back on earth. "I need some cold, hard facts, Hank. What are we looking at here? What's my next step?"

"Well, the first thing we need to know is whether your company is worth what you think it is. Find yourself a good commercial appraiser and have him give you an estimate on the valuation of Cash Drawer Technologies. Have him send that to me, and then we'll figure out our next steps. How does that sound?"

"Hmm," Larry mused, "I don't know. There are a lot of

things to consider."

Hank looked at him. "What do you mean?"

"Well, my plan was to sell my business or hand it down to the kids, and then we would give a certain amount to charitable organizations or foundations."

"Okay," said Hank, "but let me ask you something. You built this company from the ground up, right? It's your whole life. How likely do you think you are to really sell it when the time comes? I ask this because I have seen many businessmen just like you who think they are going to sell their company and retire, but every year they put it off. They don't end up selling it, they don't end up writing those checks, and they run the business till it dies, like an old car, pushing it into the used car lot on its last legs. What if you could stay in control of Cash Drawer and use the business to fund the causes you care about now?"

"You sound like my friend Jack Stock!"

"Well, if he is telling you that you can give more than you realize, then he's a very good friend. Listen, Larry, I know it's hard. Just bear with me. I am your advisor, and I am going to give you some advice: find that appraiser, then bring your CPA and attorney to the next meeting, and we will talk more then."

Larry agreed, and the calm returned to his voice as he and Ellie walked down the hall with Hank.

"I think somebody—maybe it was Rockefeller—said that people who are given a lot also have a lot of responsibility," Hank remarked.

"That wasn't Rockefeller," said Ellie, laughing but not unkindly. "It's from the Bible! 'For unto whomsoever much is given, of him shall much be required'!"

"Well, how about that! What do you make of it?" Hank asked as he walked them to the car.

"I think it means that people who are blessed with abundance have to really think hard about what to do with that money, what kind of impact they want to make. That's a heavy burden but a wonderful one to have…" Ellie trailed off.

"I agree," said Hank.

"I have been wondering what to talk about in my next Bible study class," Ellie said. "That passage is just the thing. Thank you, Hank!"

"You are very welcome." Hank turned to Larry. "What are you going to talk about?"

Larry scrunched his brows, remembering. "I am teaching the kids the parable of the Five Talents. It's always good for a lively discussion."

"How very similar," Ellie said with a smile as they waved good-bye to Hank.

Chapter 12

Talents and Trouble

That Sunday, Larry sat in front of a group of middle schoolers in the fellowship hall of the church. There was just a handful there, sitting on cafeteria benches and looking at their cell phones.

"So, there's this rich guy," he began, his booming voice breaking the students out of their texting stupor, "who is about to go on a long journey and asks his three servants to take care of his money for him while he is gone. He gives each one a different amount, 'according to their ability,' the Bible says."

"To one, he gives five talents—that's the word they used for money," he explained. "To the other he gave two. To the last one he gave just one. And he wanted all three of them to be stewards of his money. What do you think happened when he came back?"

The kids had all kinds of answers, and as Larry predicted, the conversation turned lively. He finally told them that two servants 'put the money to work'. "In other words, they invested it," Larry said. "The servant who was given five talents earned five more. And the one who had two earned two more."

"That's a hundred percent return," interjected one shrewd student. "I wish I knew where they put their money!"

"Call me when you graduate from Wharton," joked Larry.

"What did the servant who just got one talent do?" asked a seventh grade girl.

"Well, he told his boss a very interesting story. He said he was afraid to try to make it grow. He just dug a hole and put the money in the ground and then gave it right back to the man when he returned from his journey."

"Well, that's not a bad idea," said the first boy. "He was just judging the risk."

"Ah, but this is a parable, my future MBA," said Larry. "There's more than meets the eye. And let me tell you what the master said! He congratulated each of the first two and said," Larry read aloud, "Well done, good and faithful servant! You have been faithful with a few things; I will put you in charge of many things. Come and share your master's happiness!"

"What about the third one?" asked the girl.

"The master wasn't very happy with him," Larry told them. "Any of you ever heard the word *stewardship*?" Larry asked, veering off from his lesson plan.

The kids' collective blank stare propelled him further.

"The word *steward*," he said, "is really old. It dates back to medieval times. It comes from one word that means house and another word that means keeper or guardian."

"So a steward was a housekeeper?" asked the girl.

"More than that. Back in those days, the steward was the person that the master of the house trusted completely to run the home, and that included the money that was involved in running the house. When the master was away, the steward acted as the lord of the house, as if it were his own, protecting and managing all the assets, the staff, everything."

"So, the master in the story made his servants his stewards," the boy said, catching on.

"Yeah, the money wasn't theirs to begin with," the girl said as she checked the passage again. "They were just supposed to try to make it grow."

Larry was quiet for a moment and the girl continued. "And the master says to the good servants, 'You have been faithful with a few things; I will put you in charge of many things.'

What does that mean?"

Larry was still thinking about what the girl had said. "This parable is not only about money," he began, thoughtfully. "It's also about skills, abilities, talents...and faith. Like the rich man who gave his talents to his stewards, didn't Christ give you your skills and abilities and talents? If so, then you are a steward of them. So like the third servant, this parable asks if you should bury them in the ground and sit on them out of fear, or take them into the world with boldness and faith and try to increase them."

The kids talked about this until the class was over and then joined their parents. Larry, though, sat there at the table for a while, his own words ringing through his heart and his head, wondering whether this lesson was for them or for him.

Chapter 13

Farms and Bracelets

L arry sat in his office, thinking about the previous day's Sunday school class. When Jack arrived ten minutes early for their lunch appointment, Larry realized he had been sitting for a long time. He mentally admonished himself for losing track as he opened the door for Jack.

"Hello, Larry, I hope you don't mind if I change our plans a bit," said Jack, slightly out of breath. "I invited two people along that I really want you to meet. This is the only time they could fit in. Are you okay with that?"

"I think that's fine, Jack," said Larry. "The Lunch Box doesn't take reservations, but I'm sure they can squeeze us in. What's this all about?"

"You'll see," Jack replied.

The Lunch Box was indeed crowded, but Larry commandeered a booth in back while Jack waited for his friends outside. The three of them soon made their way through the maze of tables, and Jack made the introductions as they sat down.

"Larry, these are my friends Sam and Nancy Graves. They have just returned to the States after two weeks in Africa on a mission trip."

"Well, try the Brunswick Stew," Larry said, laughing. "It will cure your jet lag for sure!"

After four orders of stew were taken, Sam and Nancy launched into tales of their visit to Tanzania.

"You wouldn't believe it," said Nancy, "but even though about thirty-five percent of Tanzanians live below the poverty line, there is still much potential there."

"Yes," said Sam, "the economic potential is hard to ignore. One out of every three Tanzanians is self-employed, but only about twenty percent have a bank within an hour's walking distance of their home. And only four percent of rural farmers even have an account."

"Not only do they need money, but they also need access to that money," Nancy said plainly. "While seventy percent of Tanzanians earn some income from growing and selling crops, only one percent have ever used a loan to buy seeds, tools, or fertilizer. And this is the region that accounts for the majority of the country's agriculture!"

"What do they use for collateral for these loans?" Larry asked, entering into the discussion.

"Typical bank loan models don't really work there," Sam answered. "But there is a new thing happening. It's called microfinance...collateral is not necessary. Often these are group loans that the members themselves decide on; then they are responsible individually and jointly for paying back the loan."

"Sort of like peer pressure," Jack commented, reaching into the basket of rolls.

"In a good way!" agreed Sam. "And it has two effects: it values each entrepreneur's success, and the transparency allows for high levels of repayment."

"I saw an amazing thing," said Nancy, "when I went to one of these microlending banks. The borrowers would come in and dump this pile of crumpled-up bills on a table where a few people sat. One of them counted the money, another one made notes, and the last one slid change back across the table. These people might be poor, and they are shut out of traditional sources of credit, but here they are empowered to start and keep small businesses—and lift themselves and their families out of poverty."

"Oh and tell them about the bracelets!" Sam interjected.

"Oh yes!" Nancy smiled. "I met this woman who buys small amounts of African textiles from wholesalers and makes bracelets out of them. Then she sells them to retail buyers for a profit. She started with a loan of fifty thousand Tanzanian shillings "

"That's about thirty-five dollars," Sam explained.

"And once the original loan was repaid, she qualified for a higher loan," continued Nancy. "She repeated this cycle a bunch of times as her business expanded. Her loans grew… and now she has around six hundred fifty dollars. At this point, she has a real inventory!"

"And that," Sam finished, "drives a sustainable business. We saw it all over Dar es Salaam."

Wistful, Nancy leaned back in her chair. "It's so exciting to see someone succeed, all because of a loan."

"And taking care of that money," said Larry, who had been quiet. "They are learning how to be responsible for something that isn't theirs. There's a certain honor to that."

Sam agreed as he pulled out his cell phone and clicked on it. He passed around a picture of a beaming woman in front of colorful bolts of fabric. In her hands were ropes of beautiful bracelets. "That's the woman who Nancy was talking about," he said.

"She looks happy," said Jack, "but tired. About how far does she have to travel to make those loan payments?"

"Well, that is still a problem," Nancy answered. "She and

some of the other store owners are lucky because their businesses are in town. But the farmers are still very far away. We did hear of some innovative approaches being used in Ghana—kiosk satellite banks, point-of-sale devices, cell phone banking, that kind of thing…"

"Wait," Larry burst out. "They could really benefit from the sort of POS technology that we have here in the States. They could add money to their accounts, maybe even make loan payments right in their own backyards!"

"Hmm," Jack said, landing lightly on the idea. "That's right up your alley, Larry."

Larry smiled at him with a look Jack had seen before on others. It was the look he had been waiting for. It was a mix of wonder and intensity, and it lit up Larry's face as he turned to Jack.

"I want to see you first thing tomorrow morning. I've got an idea."

They finished their lunch and strolled back to their cars, parting amiably. Sam and Nancy promised to accept Larry's invitation to the house soon. That night, Larry sat down in his study listening to Ellie puttering in the kitchen. Long after the lights were off, he was still planning…and he didn't stop until late into the night.

This time Larry was at the board when Jack arrived at his office. On it he had written these numbers:

10M = 10 shares

30% DAF

"By George, I think you've got it!" Jack joked with Larry after a cursory glance.

"Good, I wanted to make sure I had it right because I think I know what I want to do."

Chapter 14

Barristers and Bean Counters

L arry's morning began with a brisk walk from his car to the office followed by a short phone call to Hank. "I'm just calling to make sure you got that appraiser's numbers," he said.

"Yes, Larry, I have them right here. Everything looks good. Now how about that CPA? Were you able to find one who has a background in business valuations?"

"Yes," said Larry, "actually I am going to use the accountant I have on retainer. He is already familiar with the day-to-day bookkeeping and tax filings for Cash Drawer and also knows the valuations side of things."

"That's fine, Larry. And your attorney?"

"My regular business attorney is Cynthia Stratton. She has very up-to-date experience in mergers and acquisitions and things like that. I think she will be fine. And my friend Jack.

He'll be coming, too."

"Okay then, Larry. Looks like the cast of characters is in place!" Hank joked. "Let's schedule a time for all of us to meet."

That meeting, back in the "living room" of Hank's office, was a week later on a rainy Monday.

They all sat down and began to review the figures in front of them. After a fair amount of getting up to speed, the discussion about Larry's plans began to take shape.

Hank said, "I've been looking at a DAF to transfer your business interests into and wondered what you thought about that."

"Before you answer, Mr. Rose," Cynthia said, "I just want you to know that the law allows you to retain decision-making power. Whoever controls fifty percent—plus one share—has voting rights. Giving even up to thirty percent of Cash Drawer's stock will have no impact on the governance of the company. You really would be giving up nothing."

"Except capital gains taxes," said the accountant.

"Of course. Now, at some point, I would like to hand the business down to the kids," Larry said. "How would a DAF affect that?"

"They can still be part of this," Hank assured.

"I have worked with a lot of people who have done this, Mr. Rose," the accountant said consolingly. "And they have been very pleased."

"Okay," Larry said. "That's what I needed to know. Now I'm going to tell you a little story. Back when I started my business, I got a loan from my grandfather. As soon as I was able, I paid him back and made him part of the board of trustees. You see, all that time I was building the business, I knew this wasn't my money; it was his. I wanted to honor him by taking good care of it and making the business successful. Every decision I made rested on that fact. It was quite a heavy responsibility."

Saying this last bit made Larry stop. He looked around at the assembled group. "Now," he said after a while, "I am ready to do that same thing again. But I want to make sure you are all on board with me and have the same sense of responsibility that I do. Because this thing—this is big."

"Larry, understandably, you are nervous about pulling the trigger on the DAF." Hank smiled warmly.

"No, Hank, that's not it. That's not it at all. This isn't about the money. This is much, much bigger than that." Larry opened his arms wide. "This is about changing the world!"

Chapter 15

The Three Buckets

Jack Stock sat on a bench under the pines and considered the clouds. It was about time to move on, but he had one more appointment to make. When the U-Line bus stopped in front of him, he jumped on and enjoyed the ride to the Hargraves auditorium. He made his way to a seat in the back and waited.

"Thank you all so much for being here," boomed a voice from the podium. "I am here today to tell you about an amazing adventure. And it all happened right here," said the speaker, pointing to his heart. "I am Larry Rose, and I used to think I knew what it meant to own things."

"Early in my career, I decided to own my own business. I was able to control things and know where every dollar went. I asked my grandfather for a loan, and Cash Drawer was born. And when I say born, it felt every bit like my baby."

Many people in the audience nodded their heads in agreement.

"After a long and illustrious run, and our kids had graduated from college and had their own jobs, my wife and I began to talk about my exit plan. We thought about selling the business, living off the proceeds, and giving a lot of that money to charity. But the thought of selling my baby gave me the heebie-jeebies. It would mean that I couldn't hand it down to the children, a dream of ours. And the thing that kept me up at night was the idea of retiring *period*. I wanted to have something important to do."

He paused for emphasis. "I was at a crossroads."

"And, wouldn't you know, the next thing that happened was that I met a very special person. He came along right when I was going through all of these questions and turned everything I had been thinking upside-down. He introduced me to a new concept. *Give* part of the business away. That's right, you heard me. Give it away."

"Do you think he was crazy? So did I! But this is what happened. He told me about something called a Donor-Advised Fund. Now, just think about this. You are the donor. And you advise where the funds are allocated. It sounded okay to me, so I listened."

"But, I tell you, I was not a quick study. I was resistant. I was having a hard enough time thinking of retiring. Think about how hard it was for me to think about giving it away!"

The audience laughed.

"But my friend was patient with me. He drew all kinds of diagrams and all kinds of charts and graphs, but the one that made the most sense was using my own model of how I thought about money: Two Buckets."

Larry pointed to the screen at the back of the stage and clicked the button in his hand. A slide with two buckets appeared on the screen, much like the pictures Jack had drawn in Larry's office a few years ago.

"One bucket is for lifestyle, and the other is for taxes. That's what I thought my money was all about. But I was wrong. There is a third bucket." Another slide came up. "The giving bucket. And this is what made me take the right turn at the crossroads."

"Let me tell you how it happened. I teach a Bible study class at my local church, and one day I decided to teach the story of the Five Talents in the Bible. Some of you probably know it."

Several heads nodded. For those who didn't, he gave a brief summary of the parable.

"Well," he continued, "what made that story stand out to me was that the group of middle schoolers I was teaching saw something I had missed. I always thought the moral of the story was that you shouldn't be lazy, that if someone gives you something, you should work hard to make something better out of it—you shouldn't just do nothing and put it in the ground. But that day, I had an epiphany, my friends. What was clear to the kids but not to me until that day was that I had been thinking of my business all wrong. I was thinking of it as *mine*. And one little girl in that Sunday school class said it: 'It wasn't their money; it was their master's. They were just supposed to make sure nothing happened to it.' So simple! My money wasn't mine—it had a higher purpose. I was just supposed to make sure nothing happened to it. In other words, I was a steward. I can't tell you how this changed me."

Larry stopped and took a drink of water from a bottle on the podium and started speaking again.

"So naturally I began to see things from a different vantage point. You know what I kept asking myself?"

Larry paused for effect and looked around at the audience's expectant faces.

"How can I change the world? Every decision came from that question. I knew that I had the business acumen to make a real impact on the world, to change people's lives for the better. And I began to see that I had the means as well. I was beginning to expand my idea of the world beyond my neighborhood and to see that I could reach much farther."

"Immediately I knew what I would do. It had all been coming together—I just didn't know it yet—but all the pieces were there. I knew I wanted to help people out of poverty but not just by giving them money. I wanted to use money in a way that would help people have faith in themselves and in their ability to run businesses, just the way the loan from my grandfather did for me."

"Thanks to some new friends, I learned that there were people in the country of Tanzania who were exploring a banking program called 'microlending.' Small loans are given to farmers and storeowners, and a structure is set up to help them repay the loans and qualify for more. But the borrowers needed a safe and accessible way to get and pay back the loans. So I wanted to figure out a way to get them the resources they needed to do that. And with my background, it was a short hop to the next step: develop a POS system that would put that ability right in the palms of their hands. It was a no-brainer!"

The slides on the screen changed to images of the Tanzanian farmers and shopworkers with handheld devices as Larry went on.

"Instead of selling my business—or worse—waiting to *retire*," Larry said, with his fingers making quotes in the air, "I gave a portion of my business to a donor-advised fund. They set up the transfer, and the process began!"

"Suddenly I had the same sense of purpose that I had when

I first started my business. But there was a huge shift in my thinking. And look at what was happening."

He pointed to a new slide with a drawing of the giving bucket filling up. "I won't bore you with the particulars, but if you are a business owner, you are no doubt familiar with a schedule K-1." He looked out in the audience to see general assent. "I had already enjoyed significant tax deductions as a result of gifting a portion of Cash Drawer. But what I was not prepared for was this giving, which was happening every quarter. As you know, the net profits flow through to the owners of the company. Well, Cash Drawer had two owners—the donor-advised fund and me. I was seeing on my K-1s that we had a profit of seventy-five thousand dollars going into my account at the DAF *every quarter*. This was real money! I was the steward of this money, and I had some serious decisions to make."

"I put the same passion into these decisions that I put into my business. I thought I could never feel the same way about anything as I felt about Cash Drawer, but this was even better."

"And instead of thinking of ways to keep myself busy during retirement, I found myself running the fund like I was running my business. I had to constantly ask myself how I could maximize my impact for the betterment of the world. I was charged with stewardship, as it was never my money, from that first loan from my grandfather to now. The money was never mine! I was able to use my business as a vehicle to live out my purpose in life: to make as big an impact as possible. And once I do retire, if I ever do, and hand the company down to the children, that money still goes into the giving bucket. And it will be their duty to manage it responsibly."

"Now there are villages all over Ghana and Tanzania that are able to utilize these systems, and the microlending model is really taking off, allowing rural farmers to access their accounts and pay their loans. There is a ninety-eight percent rate of payback with these new systems in place. I now split my time between Africa and the States, making sure that things run smoothly, and I still count everything. I now live my life with a sense of purpose. Through my business, I am able to impact the world in a way I could never have dreamed possible."

As Larry finished and began to take questions from the audience, Jack quietly sidestepped out of his seat and walked through the lobby of the auditorium. He entered the clear, blue Carolina afternoon and made his way to the bus stop.

He had another CEO to meet.

THE END

Resources

While this story is fiction, the concepts contained within it are not. These concepts have been used by hundreds of companies and business owners around the country. The process is fairly easy and straightforward and, with the right advice, can be executed in a relatively short period of time. One of the leaders in this effort is the National Christian Foundation (www.nationalchristian.com). It is headquartered in Atlanta, Georgia, but has chapters in a number of cities around the country.

Our goal in this book is to create a resource that Christian nonprofit development officers can use to inspire business owners to become more engaged. This requires one critical step, which results in a major outcome. That first critical step is the desire to move from success to significance— the desire on the part of the business owner to take his or her business experience, drive, skills, and talent and use them for something larger than him- or herself. Once the donor-advised fund is established and money begins flowing to this fund from the business, the business owner sees him- or herself as a steward of those funds, as opposed to an owner. This often flows over into the owner's approach to all of his or her assets. The business owner begins to understand that all money is God's, and that he or she is simply a steward for a short period of time. We've seen this outcome occur over and over again.

We hope this book will be useful in generating more resources and committed business leaders for the kingdom. We would love to hear your thoughts and suggested improvements. Please feel free to contact us at any time.

www.TheThirdBucket.com

Books

Halftime, Bob Buford

From Success to Significance: When the Pursuit of Success Isn't Enough, Lloyd Reeb

The Treasure Principle, Randy Alcorn

Generous Living, Ron Blue

Change Agent, Oz Hillman

Websites

www.halftimeinstitute.org
www.opportunity.org
www.marketplaceleaders.org

About the Authors

Richard Cope, CEO of Nanolumens (www.Nanolumens. com) is a visionary with more than twenty-five years of intense leadership experience and a track record of proven results. Cope has served as a successful CEO, president, CTO, COO, combat commander, venture capitalist, and fund-raiser. He has extensive high-tech, high-growth experience that quickly moves companies from research to sustainable revenue. His contagious, focused enthusiasm motivates people into high-performance teams, building high-energy environments, and driving bottom-line results. He has been lauded by the Hudson Institute as the creator of the best public-private partnership in history. He currently works with Opportunity International, Legacy of Truth, and other ministries.

Randy Brunson is founder and CEO of Centurion Advisory Group (www.centurionag.com), a fee-only wealth management and multifamily office firm. Brunson has invested his career in helping business owners and other high-net-worth individuals make informed decisions about their lives and money. He continues to apply and teach the strategic and tactical aspects of integrating life, money, and purpose . He currently works with Youth For Christ, and other ministries.

Dear reader,

We are interested in your feedback and encourage you to let us know how we can improve this story. Please feel free to contact either of us with your ideas.

All of the proceeds from this book will go to charitable organizations.

Richard Cope, CEO, Nanolumens
4900 Avalon Ridge Parkway
Norcross, GA 30071
Rcope@NanoLumens.com
(+1) 678.428.4090 (m)
(+1) 678.974.1535 (o)
www.nanolumens.com

Randy Brunson, CEO, Centurion Advisory Group
1532 Dunwoody Village Parkway, Suite 204
Atlanta, GA 30338
RBrunson@CenturionAG.com
(+1) 678.478.5781 (m)
(+1) 770.817.0525 (o)
www.Centurionag.com

CPSIA information can be obtained at www.ICGtesting.com
Printed in the USA
LVOW12s1028220115

423902LV00001B/1/P

9 781478 746508